The Little Stream

The Little Stream

by Barry Ellsworth

Illustrations by Steve Day

BONNEVILLE
Classic Books

A Member of Bonneville
International Corporation

ISBN: 1-56684-082-1

Third Printing

Bonneville Classic Books
55 North 300 West
Salt Lake City, Utah 84110

Printed in the United States of America.

To the American Indian

It had been a long, hot, dry, winter...

under the desert sun...

that seemed as though it would never end.

The prairie grass was gray and withered.

The flowers were no more.

And a cold hush of death lay over all the land.

Yet...

everywhere...

was a sense of hope...

and anticipation.

Finally...

one day...

above the mountains, far to the west...

a dark and ominous cloud began to form.

All day long it grew...

and grew...

until it was large and black...

filling the western sky.

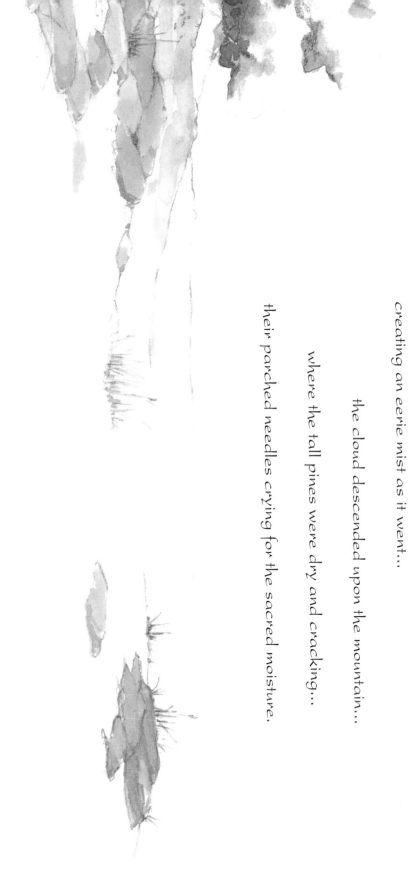

Then...

slowly...

creating an eerie mist as it went...

the cloud descended upon the mountain...

where the tall pines were dry and cracking...

their parched needles crying for the sacred moisture.

And... suddenly... it happened.

With a loud - KA BOOM

the thunder roared...

and lightning streaked across the sky.

And little drops of the sacred water...

began to fall.

Small at first...

confused...

joining with others as they fell.

Faster and faster...

until they were large...

and the downpour enveloped the mountain.

And all drank of the holy waters.

The pine, the aspen, the oak...

and the sacred Earth Herself...

deeply...

until the water filled Its belly.

And the souls of all Living things...

cried songs of praise and gratitude...

to the Great Spirit of Life...

thanking It for the holy...

life-giving waters from on high.

And they drank...

and drank...

until they could drink no more.

Yet...

still...

it rained.

And all being filled...

the water...

with nowhere else to go...

began running down the sides of the mountain...

to the valley of the mountain below.

And as the waters...

from all sides...

met on the valley floor...

a stream was formed...

that grew...

and grew.

Until...

suddenly...

it awoke!

Then....

it remembered!

It remembered it had a mission...

a purpose for coming to Earth.

And it remembered the sacred song...

the Great Spirit, the Father of all Living things...

had taught it to sing...

to help it remember its mission...

before falling from on high.

So it began to sing the song.

Give sang the little stream
Give o give
Give o give

Give sang the little stream
As it hurried down the hill

I'm small I know
But wherever I go
The grass grows greener still

Singing singing all the day
Give o give o give away

Singing singing all the day
Give o give away

And as the little stream sang...

the song brought joy to its heart.

And the little stream was happy.

So on it sang.

And as it sang, it moved...

gently...

through the valley of the mountain...

towards the parched and thirsty desert below...

giving freely...

to all it met along its way...

asking nothing in return.

It gave of its waters to the seeds of the grass...

asleep in the womb of Mother Earth.

And the seeds drank.

And as they drank...

they began to stir within the womb of their holy Mother...

until...

finally...

awakening...

they stretched the limbs of their cramped bodies...

and reached up to breathe the sacred air...

and to bask in the heat of the holy fire of the sun.

And as they awoke from their sleep, they were filled with joy.

And sang praises to the Great Spirit, the Father of all Life.

And were happy.

And the leaves of the trees...

having drunk of the waters of the little stream...

awoke...

and gently opened themselves to the wonders of life...

and whispered their praises to the Great Spirit...

as they rustled in the wind.

And they were happy.

And the songbirds came to the edge of the stream...

and bathed...

and drank...

and sang their beautiful songs for all to hear.

And they were happy, too.

And the children of the animals that lived upon the mountain…

asleep in the wombs of their mothers…

the buffalo, the antelope, the deer, and the elk…

all heard the sweet melodies of the songbirds.

And awoke.

And were born.

And were happy.

And the little stream...

saw that its work was good.

And was happy.

So on it went...

with a smile on its face...

that twinkled...

as the bright sunlight danced across its surface...

to the desert below.

And the little stream never complained.

And wasn't afraid.

Even when there were large...

rough-looking boulders in its path.

For it had a purpose...

a mission to accomplish...

given to it by the Great Spirit...

Who knew what would make

the little stream happy.

So when the little stream came upon the great, big boulders...

it didn't stop and become paralyzed with fear...

wondering what it should do next.

It simply went around them, over them...

or under them...

eventually wearing them down...

smoothing their jagged edges.

Nor was it afraid of what it couldn't see around the next bend.

For it remembered the Great Spirit's

words and promise...

given to the little stream before falling to Earth...

that nothing could stop the little stream

from accomplishing its mission in life....

that He would always be with it...

to guide it....

and clear its path before it...

and that nothing the little stream ever did...

absolutely nothing...

could ever stop the Great Spirit from loving it.

Because the Great Spirit...

loved the little stream with all of His heart...

with a love that was unchanging...

never-ending.

And the little stream loved and trusted its Father...

and the children of its Father...

And was happy.

So on it went...

fearlessly...

never complaining...

never alone...

always loved...

singing its little song.

And as the days rolled by…

the mountain became vibrant with Life.

And all Living things sang their praises…

giving thanks for the sacred waters of the little stream.

And they danced in a celebration of Life.

And were happy.

And seeing this...

brought such joy and happiness to the little stream...

that it thought it could hold no more.

Yet it knew in its heart that its work was not done.

So with a mission still, it faced down the hill...

and singing goodbye, with a gleam in its eye...

it moved on to the desert below.

On its way...

the little stream continued to give freely to all it met...

and accomplished so much.

But after doing so much good work...

it was moving a little more slowly...

because parts of the little stream were becoming tired.

So they stopped to rest.

They rested in small, dark holes at the side of the stream.

But not knowing what they were doing...

being unfamiliar with dark holes...

sometimes...

they got stuck.

When they did they became dark like the holes...

isolated, frightened...

stagnant and sick.

And they tried as best they could...

to get out of the little holes.

And some of them did.

And they were relieved as they joined the stream again.

For as they moved within the stream...

they were cleansed of their sickness...

purified and revitalized.

And they taught the rest of the little stream...

not to do what they had done.

They said the small, dark holes were scary....

and that if they stayed in them too long...

they'd become dark like the holes...

and get stagnant and sick.

They said it was better to stick together...

within the stream as One...

to just keep moving....

be happy and thankful...

and stay out of the little, black holes.

And this made the little stream happy.

However, some of the water never got out of the little, black holes.

It tried and it tried with all of its might...

but couldn't escape.

And this was sad.

But the Great Spirit...

seeing this...

kept His promise to the little stream.

For the Great Spirit, the Giver of all Life...

loves and cares for each and every one of His children.

And not one drop of the little stream was left unnoticed.

So He sent the heat...

of the holy fire of the sun...

to shine upon the parts of the little stream...

that had become stuck and sick.

And the heat of the sun...

caused them to rise into the sacred air...

where the Great Spirit breathed them

into His heart again.

And they were home.

And they were happy.

And after having quietly observed all of these many things...

being careful to judge nothing that occurred...

as good or bad...

as its Father had taught it to do...

the surface of the little stream had become so still and tranquil...

that its waters had turned into a great mirror...

in which the truth of all that had taken place...

was so clearly reflected...

that the little stream was actually able...

to bless the darkness...

and the lessons learned from it...

as easily as it was the light.

For in the peace and clarity of its tranquil mind...

caused by its refusal to judge anything...

the little stream was able to discern...

that all things created by the Great Spirit...

were truly connected...

and had a reason for being.

And that there were no accidents

in the Great Spirit's loving plan for His children...

just bright, new chances to learn and to grow.

And this made the little stream happy.

Finally...

the little stream reached the desert floor.

And all Living things...

drank of the little stream's sacred waters.

And Life was renewed in the desert.

The prairie grass drank...

and lifted its weary head...

and blew in the breeze.

And was happy.

The seeds of the desert flowers drank…

and stirred within the womb of their sacred Mother…

and stretched and reached and grew…

and turned their joyous, happy faces towards the heavens…

and gave thanks to the Great Spirit…

with the blazing colors of their splendor.

For their long sleep had ended.

Their thirst had been quenched.

And they were happy.

And the buffalo, the antelope, the deer, and the elk…

all came to the desert with their children…

to partake of the prairie grass…

and be nourished and fed.

And to drink again of the holy waters of the little stream.

And they were filled.

And they were happy.

And their children were happy, too.

And they danced and frolicked and kicked...

and played with one another...

in a celebration of Life.

And this made the little stream happy.

And because the little stream was so happy...

and had stayed so busy...

because it had found such joy in the love of its work...

and service to others...

it hadn't noticed, its days had turned to weeks...

its weeks, to the months of summer and fall.

Because it was just too happy.

For the little stream had given...

freely...

to all Living things.

And all had drunk of the little stream's sacred waters...

and been filled.

And all had known the Joy of Life.

And had danced and sang in Its celebration.

And all were happy.

nd the little stream never complained.

And wasn't afraid.

And with a smile on its face...

that twinkled as the light of the desert moon...

danced across its surface...

being happy and thankful...

with a song in its heart...

never alone...

judging not...

and always loved...

it just kept moving...

and moving...

and moving...

Until...

it was...

no more.

And the winter came...

And for a very, very long time...

it was hot and dry...

under the desert sun.

Then...

one day...

above the mountains...

far to the west...

The End

Acknowledgments

I'd like to take these few lines to thank and acknowledge some of the people and places... which have deeply influenced my life and thinking.

My mother and father — for my life and their unfailing love.

My brothers and sister, and the sweet attentions of their children.

Colt and Cache — for the love we've shared with one another.

Mark and Toni — for their friendship and constant support over the years.

Chris Harding — whose vision and love for the story made this book a reality.

The profound wisdom of the American Indian... as well as that of Anne Naess, George Sessions, and Lynn White Jr.

The majesty of Boulder Mountain... the spiritual magic of the canyons of Pleasant Creek... and the deserts of Capital Reef National Monument.

Fanny Crosby, who wrote the words, and William Bradbury, who wrote the music... to the original version of the song... Give Said the Little Stream... sometime before 1868.

And Beverly Lindholm, my Sunday School teacher... who at the age of 19 or 20, taught the song to me, when I was but four... and who later that very same year, absolutely broke my little heart when she married another man.